THE SECRET
OF THE SCROLL

Adapted by
J. E. Bright

📕 HarperEntertainment
An Imprint of HarperCollinsPublishers

CHAPTER ONE

Legend tells of a fighter who had unbeatable kung fu skills.

The warrior traveled the land righting wrongs and protecting the innocent.

One day, in a small, remote restaurant, the warrior was drinking tea and chewing bamboo. The door blasted open and the filthy Manchu Pig Gang rushed in to surround him. "I see you like to chew!" the boss pig hollered. "Maybe you should chew on my fist!" The boss pig punched the table.

The warrior didn't reply because his mouth was full. Finally, he swallowed. "Enough talk," he said. "Let's fight!" With a single punch, the warrior sent

1

the entire Manchu Pig Gang flying across the restaurant. Then, one hundred assassins dropped out of the ceiling and encircled the warrior. "Shashabooey!" the warrior bellowed. He spun like a tornado, blasting the roof off the restaurant and sending a funnel of ninjas spurting into the sky. His enemies went blind from overexposure to his pure awesomeness.

The warrior stood amidst his defeated foes, rays of sunlight shining down upon him. Even the most awesome kung fu warriors in all of China, the Furious Five, bowed in respect to him. But there was no time to bask in the glory. The warrior pulled out a giant sword and pointed it toward a new group of attacking foes. There were still wrongs to right, innocence to protect . . . and butts to kick.

Suddenly Po landed on a hard floor, waking from his dream. He stared up at the action figures of his favorite kung fu heroes displayed around his bedroom.

The portly panda rocked on his back, trying to kick himself onto his feet. But his potbelly made that impossible.

"Po, what are you doing up there?" his father yelled.

"Nothing!" Po replied. He struggled upright, and then struck poses like the Furious Five. "Monkey! Mantis!" he huffed, announcing his heroes' names. "Crane! Viper! Tigress!"

"Po, let's go!" his father shouted. "You'll be late for work!"

"Okay!" Po called back. First, though, he picked up a ninja star from the floor and chucked it at the wall. It bounced off. Po tried to fling the star into the wall again, but it plunked onto the floor. He grabbed it and stuffed it into his back pocket. Then Po headed downstairs, tripping and falling on the steps all the way to the bottom.

"You're late," Po's father, a scrawny goose, reprimanded him. He put down the baskets of noodles he had been carrying.

Po hopped to his feet in a warrior's stance.

"Sorry, Dad," he said. "I was having the craziest dream."

"Yeah?" his father asked. "What were you dreaming about?"

"Um . . ." Po felt silly explaining his kung fu dream to his father. He wouldn't understand. "I was dreaming . . . uh . . . about noodles." He took the throwing star out of his pocket and quickly stuffed it back in—jabbing himself in the butt.

Po's father was too excited to notice the throwing star. "My son, finally having the noodle dream!" he exclaimed. "Po, you are almost ready to learn the secret ingredient of my Secret Ingredient Soup. Then you will take over this restaurant, just as I took it over from my father, who took it over from his father, who won it in a game of mahjong."

"Dad," Po asked, "didn't you ever want to do something else, besides making noodles?"

A wistful look misted his father's eyes. "No, we all have our place in this world. Mine is here. And yours—"

"I know," Po replied dutifully. "Mine is here, too."

"Actually, it's at table three," his father said. "You're late with their order."

As Po clumsily carried a tray of food through the crowded noodle shop, apologizing for bumping into customers, he glanced outside. Up on a majestic mountain stood the Jade Palace, gleaming in the sunlight. Po was mesmerized.

The Jade Palace was the place of kung fu dreams, where the Furious Five trained to protect the Valley of Peace. It was the place of the legendary Dragon Scroll, which would be given only to the legendary Dragon Warrior.

To Po in the noodle shop, the Jade Palace on its mountain felt very far away.

CHAPTER TWO

Later that morning, messengers from the palace arrived in town. They hung up posters announcing that a competition to choose the new Dragon Warrior would be held that afternoon. When Po saw a poster in his father's noodle shop, he excitedly rushed into the kitchen to find his father.

"Dad!" he cried. "We've got to get up to the Jade Palace! One of the Five is gonna get the Dragon Scroll! We've been waiting a thousand years for this!"

Po started to run.

"Po! Where are you going?"

"To the Jade Palace," Po said quietly.

"You're forgetting your cart. The whole valley is going to be there, and you'll sell noodles to all of them!" he finished.

"Selling noodles? But, Dad!"

That afternoon, throngs of villagers filed up the stairs to the Jade Palace to watch the competition. At the bottom of the long, long, *long* path of stairs, Po stared up at the difficult climb ahead of him. He already felt hot in his hat and apron.

For a few minutes, Po struggled to push the noodle cart up the steps.

"Sorry, dude," a sporty pig commented, chuckling, as he and another pig hurried past Po on the staircase. "We'll bring you back a souvenir."

Po's eyes narrowed as the pigs ran up the stairs ahead of him. He stood up. "No," he said firmly, "*I'll* bring me back a souvenir."

Peeling off his hat and apron, Po took a deep breath and again began climbing up the long flight of stairs—this time without his cart.

Finally, Po hoisted himself over the top step, gasping for air. He laughed victoriously as he flopped down in front of the arena. "Yeah!" he cheered.

Just then, the arena doors began to close.

"No!" Po shouted. "Wait, I'm coming!" He heaved himself up and ran to the entrance. The doors shut in his face, so he pounded on them. "Hey, open up!" he bellowed, but his voice was drowned out by the thumping of loud drums.

"Let me in!" Po yelled. But the audience's cheers overwhelmed his shout.

Po spotted a high, open window in the wall and hurried over to it. He jumped up and struggled to pull himself high enough to see into the arena.

Master Shifu, the kung fu instructor at the Jade Palace, stood at the edge of a center ring, addressing the crowd. "Citizens of the Valley of Peace, it is my great honor to present to you the Furious Five! Tigress! Viper! Crane! Monkey! Mantis!"

Po watched through the window as his five heroes jumped into the ring and struck fighting poses. He got only a glimpse before a strong gust of wind knocked Po to the ground and slammed the window shut.

He ran over to a crack in the wall. "Peeky hole!" he cheered, peering onto the field to see Crane spreading his wings, preparing for a flight attack. But then a member of the crowd on the other side of the wall blocked his view. When Po stepped back to look over the wall to see Crane in the sky, his

paw slipped on
the top edge
of the stairs.
He fell down
the steps and
climbed up
again in time
to hear the crowd
cheering Crane's
amazing move.

He was missing
everything! It was time to get
serious about gaining entry into the
arena. Po tried to use a long pole to vault
over the wall, but he fell onto his back and the
pole whipped him on the butt. Beyond the wall,
the crowd cheered another incredible move.

Po noticed a rope hanging from a tree. He
pulled the rope, bending the tree. When the tree
had flexed enough, it launched Po into the air
like a slingshot. As he flew up and over the arena,
he caught a peek of Tigress preparing to deliver
a vicious blow. Then he fell out of view, landing
outside a tent on the other side of the wall.

Po could hear the legendary Master Oogway say,

"I sense the Dragon Warrior is among us." Master Oogway was an ancient turtle who had protected the Valley of Peace for generations and who had even trained Master Shifu.

"Citizens of the Valley of Peace, Master Oogway will now choose the Dragon Warrior!" Shifu announced.

"Wait!" Po cried. He sat up and saw that the cart next to him was filled with fireworks for the celebration. He quickly tied a bristling bunch of fireworks to a chair.

Po hopped on the chair and lit the fuse.

CHAPTER THREE

"Po!" his father cried. "What are you doing?" His father ran over and tried to blow out the burning fuse.

"Stop!" Po shouted. "I'm going to see the Dragon Warrior!"

"I don't understand," his father said. "What about the noodle dream?"

Po grabbed on to the chair and closed his eyes. "I don't dream about noodles, Dad!" he declared. "I love kung fu!"

After a pause, Po opened his eyes again, expecting to be airborne. But he was still on the ground. The fuse was a dud. Po blushed in embarrassment.

His father held out an apron. "Come on, son," he said. "Let's go back to work."

"Okay," Po agreed with a sigh. He reached out for the apron.

BOOM! The fireworks' rockets ignited, blasting him into the sky.

"Come back!" Po's father screamed.

Po soared above the arena wall, trailing sparks behind him. The crowd gasped at the display while Po shot higher and higher . . . until the rockets lost power. Then he started to fall.

"Uh-oh," Po muttered. He plummeted toward the field below.

Po crashed on the ground in front of his heroes, blasting up a big cloud of dirt.

When the dust settled, Po was amazed to see Master Oogway pointing at him and smiling. "Where . . . What's going on?" he sputtered. "Oh, okay, sorry . . . I just wanted to see who the Dragon Warrior was. . . ."

"How interesting," Master Oogway said. Po tried to scuttle out of the way, but the old turtle's finger followed him.

Master Oogway shuffled forward and grabbed Po's paw, holding it up for all to see. "The universe has brought us the Dragon Warrior!"

Po, Shifu, and the Furious Five all gasped in

disbelief, but the crowd went berserk, throwing confetti all around the arena. Palace geese rushed over and strained to lift Po up on a ceremonial litter.

Shifu pushed his way through the crowd to speak to Oogway. "Wait, that flabby panda can't possibly be the answer to our problem. Please, you were about to point at Tigress. That thing fell in front of her. That was just an accident!"

"There are no accidents," Master Oogway replied with a smile.

CHAPTER FOUR

Po was carried into the ornate Jade Palace and set down in the Sacred Hall of Heroes. Left alone, Po wandered down the hall, noticing all the legendary kung fu artifacts. Shifu was waiting for him in the Scroll Room.

"So, you're the legendary Dragon Warrior, hmm?" the tiny red panda growled.

"Uh, I guess so," Po replied.

Shifu shook his head. "Wrong!" he declared. "You will not be the Dragon Warrior until you have learned the secret of the Dragon Scroll." He pointed up at the high ceiling, where a giant carved dragon held the scroll in its impressive jaws.

Po gaped up at the famous scroll. "Wow . . . so how does this work? You have a ladder or a trampoline or—"

"You think I'm just going to hand you the secret to limitless power?" Shifu asked. "One must first master the highest level of kung fu. That is clearly impossible for someone like you." Shifu slowly circled the panda. "Look at you," he sneered, poking Po with his staff. "This fat butt. These flabby arms. This ridiculous belly."

"Listen," Po argued, shaking his finger at Shifu, "Oogway said that I was the—"

Lightning fast, Shifu reached out and snagged Po's finger in a firm pinch.

"Not the Wuxi Finger Hold!" Po cried.

"Developed by Master Wuxi in the Third Dynasty—"

"Oh, you know this hold?" Shifu replied.

"Then you must know what happens when I flex my pinkie. The hardest part is cleaning up afterward."

"Okay, take it easy," Po pleaded.

"Now listen closely, panda," Shifu hissed. "Oogway may have picked you, but when I'm through with you, you're going to wish he hadn't. Are we clear?"

"We're clear," Po promised. "We are so clear."

"Good," Shifu said. "I can't wait to get started."

Shifu let go of Po's finger and led him to the training hall. Po was amazed to see the Furious Five performing death-defying kung fu moves in the middle of a busy obstacle course. He stared in awe as Tigress smashed a ball of spiked wood into tiny shards.

"Let's begin," Shifu said.

"Now?" Po asked nervously, glancing around at the dangerous-looking training equipment. "I don't know if I can do all those moves. Maybe we can find something more suited to my level?"

Shifu shook his head. "There is no such thing as level zero."

Po pointed at a training dummy that looked a little safer than the others. "Maybe I can start with that."

"We use that for training children," Shifu said scornfully, "and for propping open the door when it's hot."

The Furious Five gathered around Po, which made him feel very nervous. He approached the dummy carefully, trying to psych himself up. He punched it lightly. It rocked back into place.

"Why don't you try again? A little harder . . ."

Po hit the dummy again, this time knocking it all the way backward. He turned around and gave Shifu a smug smile. "How's that?"

But before Po could say anything else, the dummy rocked back up and smacked him on the back of the head. Dazed, Po stumbled through the obstacle course. A spiky, tethered ball whacked him into a big bowl shaped like a turtle, where he spun around until he felt like barfing. He spilled out of the turtle bowl, tumbling into an army of wooden dummies. The last dummy whapped him in the crotch.

"Ooh, my tenders," Po moaned, collapsing to the floor.

He pulled himself upright using a dummy's arm. The dummy flipped him back into the obstacle course, where he got battered and bruised all over again. He nearly caught on fire as he stumbled through a section of the floor that shot out flames.

Singed and beaten, Po crawled toward
Shifu and the Furious Five. "How did I do?"
he whimpered.

"There is now a level zero,"
Shifu replied.

CHAPTER FIVE

That night, Po wandered around the bunkhouse looking for a place to sleep. Nobody had assigned him a bedroom, and he wasn't sure where to go. Everyone else's rooms were already dark. Although he tried to be quiet, Po's footsteps creaked as he roamed the halls. He was trying so hard to step silently that he lost his balance, and tumbled through a bedroom door.

Po opened his eyes to see Crane staring back at him from his bed. "Oh, hi," Po said. "You're up."

"I am now," Crane replied. "I've had a long day, so I should probably get to sleep now."

"Of course," Po said. "It's just . . . aw, man, I'm such a big fan. You guys were totally awesome at the Battle of Weeping River! Hi-YAH!" Po attempted a series of goofy chops and kicks, but only ended up putting his paw through one of the room's paper walls. Monkey peered out from his own room, looking very annoyed. "Sorry about that," Po apologized.

"Look," Crane said firmly, "you don't belong here."

Po lowered his head, feeling hurt to hear that from one of his heroes. "You got me. I'm just a fat, clumsy panda."

"I mean you don't belong in this room," Crane interrupted. "This is *my* room."

"Okay," Po said, backing out into the hallway. "Good night. Sleep well."

In the hall, Po let out a big sigh and resumed tiptoeing around, searching for a vacant place to lie down. Behind him, another door opened, and Tigress glared out at him. "You don't belong here," she growled.

"Oh yeah," Po said. "This is your room."

"No," Tigress clarified. "I mean you don't belong in the Jade Palace at all. You're a disgrace to kung fu, and if you have any respect for who we are and what we do, you'll be gone by morning."

Po looked around to see that all five of the famous warriors were glaring at him from their doorways. Then they all closed their doors, leaving Po alone.

His shoulders slumped. "I'm a big fan," he whispered, before slinking out of the bunkhouse.

Outside, Po stopped under a peach tree and dejectedly munched on peaches.

"I see you found the Sacred Peach Tree of Heavenly Wisdom," a voice said from behind him.

Po spun around, peach juice dribbling down his chin. Master Oogway was standing in the moonlight. "I'm so sorry," Po said with his mouth full. "I thought it was just a regular peach tree."

The ancient turtle nodded. "I understand," he said. "You eat when you are upset."

"I'm not upset," Po argued. "Who said I was upset?"

"So why are you upset?" Oogway persisted. "Isn't being here what you've always wanted?"

Po swallowed, realizing it was useless to lie. "I probably was worse today at kung fu than anybody else ever in the history of kung fu."

"Probably," Oogway agreed.

"And the Furious Five," Po continued. "They totally hate me."

"Totally," Oogway replied.

"So how is Shifu ever going to turn me into the Dragon Warrior? Maybe I should just quit and go back to making noodles."

"There is a saying: Yesterday is history, tomorrow is a mystery, but today is a gift. That is why it is called the present."

As he turned to leave, Master Oogway hit the peach tree with his staff.

A ripe peach fell right into Po's open paw.

CHAPTER SIX

The next morning, when Shifu and the Furious Five arrived at the training room, Po was already there. He was struggling, sweating, and groaning as he attempted to free his legs from a split.

"You're stuck," Shifu noticed.

"Yeah, I'm stuck," Po admitted.

After Crane helped Po up, Shifu asked with a laugh, "You actually thought you could learn to do a full split in one night? It takes years to develop one's flexibility and years longer to apply it in combat."

Shifu flung two boards in the air. To Po's amazement, Tigress leaped up and executed a perfect split kick, splintering one board with each paw.

"There is only one way to learn how to fight," Shifu said, "and that is to fight."

First, Viper faced off with Po. When the panda said he was ready, Viper lashed her tail around Po's wrist, wrenched his arm backward, flung him into the air, and whipped him back down again. Po crashed on his head.

"That was awesome!" Po cheered, giving Viper a salute. "Let's do it again!"

Next up was Monkey,

who beat Po to a pulp with a bamboo staff. Once again, Po acted pleased with the beating and saluted the simian.

Shifu stepped in. "I've been taking it easy on you, but no more!" Shifu threatened. "Your next opponent will be me. Step forth!"

Po came forward, and Shifu whirled him around and flattened him on the floor with his arm pinned behind him. "The true path to victory is to find your opponent's weakness," Shifu instructed, "and make him suffer for it."

"Oh, yeah!" Po hooted, delighted by what he was learning.

Po's cheerful attitude was really getting on Shifu's nerves. He whipped Po around again, trapping him in a painful finger hold. "To take his strength and use it against him," Shifu barked, "until he finally falls or quits."

Shifu's words only inspired the panda. "A real warrior never quits!" Po promised. "Don't worry, master, I will never quit!"

Frustrated, Shifu flung Po up into the air and nailed him with a flying kick. Po crashed through a door and tumbled down the long flight of steps to the valley below.

That evening in the bunkhouse, while Monkey meditated and Crane practiced calligraphy, Viper helped Mantis give Po acupuncture. The small insect stuck long needles into the panda's body to relieve all the aches and pains from the day's rough workout. Po grimaced in pain as Mantis jabbed him. "I thought you said acupuncture would make me feel *better*," he complained.

"Sorry," Mantis replied. "It's not easy finding nerve points under all this—"

"Fat?" Po supplied.

"Fur," Mantis claimed. "I was going to say fur."

"Sure you were," Po said. "I know Master Shifu is trying to inspire me, but if I didn't know any better, I'd say he was trying to get rid of me."

Viper chuckled awkwardly.

"I know he can seem kind of heartless," Mantis said, poking Po with another needle, "but he wasn't always like that."

"According to legend," Viper added, "there was once a time when Master Shifu actually used to smile. But that was before . . ."

"Before what?" Po asked.

Just then Tigress entered the bunkhouse. "Before Tai Lung," she finished.

Crane looked up from his calligraphy. "We're not really supposed to talk about him," he scolded.

"I know about Tai Lung," Po said. "He was a student, the first ever to master the thousand scrolls . . . and then he turned bad, and now he's in jail."

"He wasn't just a student," Tigress explained. "Shifu found him as a cub and raised him as a son. When Tai Lung showed talent in kung fu, Shifu trained him. He believed in him and told him he was destined for greatness. But it was never enough for Tai Lung. He wanted the Dragon Scroll, but that was not his destiny. So Tai Lung tried to take the scroll by force. Shifu had to destroy what he had created."

Tigress continued
with the story of
Tai Lung's attack on the
Jade Palace. The vicious,
powerful snow leopard
had ransacked a village
on the way up the
mountain. When he
crashed through
the palace doors,
Shifu and Oogway
were waiting for him
in the Scroll Room,
and Shifu immediately
attacked him with a kick. But because
he cared for the snow leopard, Shifu pulled
his kick short. Tai Lung didn't show the same
mercy—he countered with a devastating strike
that broke Shifu's leg.

Tai Lung lunged for the Dragon Scroll, but
Oogway stopped him cold with swift strikes
to his pressure points.

"Shifu loved Tai Lung like he'd never loved
anyone before," Tigress finished sadly. "Or
since."

Tigress looked so crestfallen
that everyone in the room
remained silent.

Finally, Tigress shook her head, clearing away the memories. "Now he has a chance to make things right, to train the *true* Dragon Warrior. But he's stuck with *you*," she snapped at Po. "A big, dumb panda who treats it all like a joke."

Po made a silly, googly-eyed face. *"Doieeee,"* he simpered.

The goofy face infuriated Tigress. "Oh! That is it!" she screamed, charging at Po.

Mantis quickly stepped between them, stopping Tigress. "My fault!" Mantis cried. "I accidentally tweaked his facial nerve."

Po fell facedown onto the floor. His back was covered with acupuncture needles.

CHAPTER SEVEN

"It's . . . *delicious*," Viper whispered. Po had cooked soup for everyone in the Jade Palace's kitchen, and now they were all sitting around a table enjoying it. "Well, if you love my Secret Ingredient Soup," Po said with a smile, "you'll really love my dad's. He actually knows the secret ingredient."

"Po, you're really good at something," Mantis said. "Why aren't you doing *that* instead of trying something you're . . ."

"Terrible at?" Po finished for him.

"No," Mantis replied. "I was going to say . . ." Then he nodded. "Yeah, terrible at. That's what I was going to say."

"You really are," Crane added gently.

"Well," Po answered, "I've been making noodles since I was three. I've been doing kung fu for only a week. I've got the rest of my life to become just like you." He raised his soup bowl for a sip, and when he lowered it, a noodle hung under his nose like a mustache.

Monkey snickered.

"You look just like Master Shifu!" Mantis exclaimed.

Po furrowed his brow, imitating Shifu. "You will never be the Dragon Warrior unless you lose five hundred pounds and brush your teeth!" When the Furious Five laughed, Po added in Shifu's voice, "What is that *noise* you're making? Laughter? I never heard of it!"

The Furious Five suddenly fell silent. "Hey, I thought my imitation was pretty good," Po said.

"It's Shifu," Monkey whispered.

"Of course it's Shifu," Po replied. "Who do you think I'm doing?"

Then Po turned his head and saw Master Shifu standing behind him, holding Master Oogway's staff.

"You think this is funny?" Shifu demanded angrily. "Tai Lung has escaped from prison and you're acting like children!" He glared at Po. "Tai

Lung is coming for the Dragon Scroll, and you're the only one who can stop him, Po!"

Po laughed. "Here I was saying you've got no sense of humor!" he said with a giggle. When Shifu didn't change his expression, Po started getting scared. "You're serious? Master Oogway will stop him—he did it before."

"No," Shifu said solemnly. He held up Oogway's staff. "Oogway cannot. Not anymore. It was his time."

Po and the Furious Five were deeply saddened by the terrible news. The master was gone.

"Our only hope is the Dragon Warrior," Shifu continued. "The panda."

Tigress stepped forward. "Master, please," she begged Shifu. "Let us stop Tai Lung. This is what you trained us for."

"No, it is not your destiny to defeat Tai Lung," Shifu replied. "It is *his*—"

He pointed at Po . . . but Po was gone. He was already running away from the Jade Palace, screaming in terror. He almost reached the top of the stairs before Shifu leaped in front of him.

"You cannot leave!" Shifu insisted. "A real warrior never quits!"

"Come on!" Po argued. "How am I supposed to beat Tai Lung? I can't even beat you to the stairs."

"You will beat him because you are the Dragon Warrior!" Shifu declared.

"You don't believe that!" Po yelled back. "From the first moment I got here, you've been trying to get rid of me!"

Shifu didn't disagree. "Yet you stayed," he replied, "because deep down inside, you believed Oogway was right."

"No!" Po shouted. "I stayed because the way you trained me hurt terribly, but it could never hurt more than it hurt every day of my life just being me." He turned his head to look at the valley below. "Down there I'm the fat, clumsy panda everyone laughs at. I don't fit in."

"I can train you," Shifu promised. "I will turn you into the Dragon Warrior."

"Yeah, how?" Po demanded.

Shifu hesitated. "I . . . don't know."

"That's what I thought," Po said, as he turned to walk back toward the Jade Palace. "You can believe all you want, but you can't change me into something I'm not."

CHAPTER EIGHT

Just before dawn the next morning, Po was busy stuffing his face in the kitchen when Shifu found him there. Shifu looked around at the mess Po had made—doors had been smashed, locks broken, and cabinets unhinged.

"What?" Po asked with his mouth full. "I eat when I'm upset, okay?"

Shifu smiled, his eyes twinkling as though he had a sudden idea. "Oh, no need to explain," Shifu replied. "I just thought you might be Monkey . . . he hides his almond cookies on the top shelf." Then the master stepped out of the kitchen.

Po wanted those almond cookies.

Without even thinking, he leaped to the top of the high cabinets and found the treats. He had to stretch his legs in an awkward position in order to reach the cookie jar, but he got the cookies. They were scrumptious.

When Shifu came back into the kitchen, Po whispered, "Don't tell Monkey," through a mouthful of cookie.

Shifu grinned up at him. "Look at you," he said.

"Yeah, I know," Po replied sadly. "I disgust you."

"No, no," Shifu said quickly. "I mean, how did you get up there?"

Po realized just how high he had climbed. "I don't know," he answered. "I guess I . . . I was getting a cookie . . ." He looked at the cookie he was holding in his paw and then stuffed it into his mouth.

"You are ten feet off the ground," Shifu pointed out, "and you have done a perfect split."

Po realized Shifu was right—his awkward leg position was a split! He'd performed the difficult move without even thinking about it. "No," Po said, "this was just an accident." Now that he was aware of his pose, Po wobbled and fell with a crash to the floor.

"There are no accidents," Master Shifu said. "Come with me."

Shifu led Po up through the mountains on a long, difficult journey to a remote location. They stopped beside a hazy pool. "This is the Pool of Sacred Tears," Shifu explained. "Here Oogway unraveled the mysteries of harmony and focus. This is the birthplace of kung fu."

Po looked around in awe. He could imagine Oogway standing in the mists, perfecting his elegant martial art.

They continued past the pool into an open field. "When you concentrate on kung fu," Shifu announced, "you're terrible. But perhaps that is my fault. I cannot train you the same way I trained the Furious Five. I now see that the way to get through to you is with . . . this!" He held up a steaming bowl of soup.

"Awesome," Po said, "because I'm hungry."

Shifu laughed. "Good. When you have been trained, you may eat. Let us begin."

All morning and late into the afternoon, Shifu ran Po through intensive training. With the incentive of the noodle soup, Po was much better at deep breathing, balance tests, push-ups, sit-ups, rock climbing, and many other kinds of exercises. It was amazing what he could accomplish with the promise of the right reward.

Finally, Shifu decided that Po had trained enough. He set a bowl of dumplings down on a boulder. "After you, panda," he said. "I vowed to train you . . . and you have been trained. You are free to eat."

Po hungrily grabbed a dumpling with his chopsticks. As he raised it to his mouth, Shifu used his own chopsticks to snatch the dumpling away and eat it.

"Hey!" Po complained.

"I said you are free to eat," Shifu repeated. "Have a dumpling."

But each time Po was about to munch a
dumpling, Shifu snagged it, eating it himself.
Their contest became more and more aggressive,
dumplings flying everywhere, until finally Po beat
Shifu to the final one.

Shifu smiled, pleased
with his pupil's progress.

Po stared at the
dumpling he had won.
Then he tossed it into
Shifu's open paw.
"I'm not hungry . . .
master," he said
humbly.

Solemnly, both Shifu and Po bowed deeply to each other.

That evening, as they returned to the Jade Palace, Po walked with an easy spring in his step.

"You have done well, panda," Shifu said.

"Done well?" Po replied. "I've done *awesome*!"

"The mark of a true hero is humility," Shifu scolded, but then he softened. "Yes, you have done awesome." He punched Po playfully on the arm. They both laughed as Crane appeared in the clouds behind them, carrying the rest of the Five on his back and crashing in a heap.

Their laughter cut off as they saw the heap of twisted bodies on the hallway floor. It was the Furious Five. None of them was moving, their shapes tangled in bizarre positions.

"Guys!" Po called. He ran over to the warriors. "They're dead? No, they're breathing. Asleep? No, their eyes are open. . . ."

Shifu scowled. There was only one warrior who could have done this. "Tai Lung has gotten stronger," he said.

Shifu busily freed the warriors' bodies.

"I thought we could stop him," Tigress growled in a mangled voice.

"Why didn't he kill us?" Viper wondered. "He could have."

Shifu stretched out the snake. "So you could come back here and strike fear in our hearts," he answered. "But it won't work!"

"It might," Po added in a shaky voice. "I'm pretty scared."

"You can defeat him, panda," Shifu declared.

"No," Po replied. "Are you kidding? They can't . . . and they're five *masters*. I'm just one *me*."

Shifu put his paw on Po's shoulder and squeezed reassuringly. "But you have one thing that no one else does . . . ," the master told him.

CHAPTER NINE

Shifu led the group into the Scroll Room and picked up Oogway's staff. He carried it over to a reflecting pool and bowed his head. Then he raised the staff into the air. Po and the Furious Five watched in amazement as peach blossom petals flickered up out of the pool and spun in the air, rising toward the carved dragon on the ceiling. The gentle tornado of blossoms knocked the tube containing the scroll out of the dragon's mouth. The tube fell, and Shifu caught it with the end of Oogway's staff.

The master held the tube out to Po. "Behold the Dragon Scroll," he said solemnly. "It is yours."

"Wait," Po said nervously. "What happens when I read it?"

"No one knows," Shifu answered, "but legend says you will be able to hear a butterfly's wings beat. You will be able to see light in the deepest cave and feel the universe in motion around you."

"Cool!" Po cheered. "Can I punch through walls? Do a quadruple backflip? Be invisible?"

"Focus!" Shifu warned. "Read the scroll, Po, and fulfill your destiny!"

Po took a deep breath and then grasped the tube and tried to pull the top off. It didn't budge. He struggled with it, tried to bite the end off, but he couldn't open it.

Shifu sighed and held out his paw. When Po passed him the tube, Shifu popped the top off effortlessly and gave it back to the panda.

"I probably loosened it up for you," Po said, as he unrolled the scroll. Golden light bathed his face as he scanned the shiny parchment.

Po let out a terrified, piercing scream. "It's blank!" he shrieked. "Here, look!" He tried to show Shifu the scroll.

Shifu averted his eyes. "No, I'm forbidden to look upon—" But he peeked. Then he grabbed the scroll. Astonished, he turned it around and upside down. "Blank?" he whispered. "I don't understand."

"Face it!" Po yelled. "Oogway picked me by accident. Of course I'm not the Dragon Warrior."

Nobody argued with him. The warriors just stood there, staring at the scroll, their mouths hanging open in shock. Shifu rolled the scroll up again, put it in its tube, and gave it back to Po. "Run. Run as fast as you can and as far as your legs will carry you."

Po accepted the tube with a short bow.

"The rest of you," Shifu instructed, "go evacuate the valley. Protect the villagers from Tai Lung's rage. When he comes, I will fight him. I can hold him off long enough for everyone to escape."

"But he'll kill you," Po said quietly.

"Then I will finally have paid for my mistake," Shifu replied. "It is time for you to continue your journey without me. I am . . . very proud to have been your master." He saluted his pupils and turned away.

Not knowing what else to do, Po returned to the village, passing all the animals as they evacuated their homes. He walked toward his father's noodle shop, devastated.

Po's father rushed out and enveloped his son in a big hug. When Po bent over to hug his dad back, he realized that his father had tied an apron around his waist. "Good to have you back, son!" his father exclaimed.

"Good to be back," Po replied listlessly.

His father packed up some belongings, preparing to leave. "The future of noodles is dice-cut vegetables, no longer sliced," his father said. "At first we'll be laughed at, but so has every pioneer."

Then Po's father realized that Po was standing still, looking very sad. He took both of Po's paws in his. "I'm sorry things didn't work out," his father said sympathetically. "It just wasn't meant to be. Your destiny still awaits. We are noodle folk—broth runs deep in our veins."

"I know, Dad," Po whispered.

Po's father took a deep breath. "I think it's time I told you something I should have told you a long time ago . . .

the secret ingredient in my Secret Ingredient Soup." He beckoned Po to lean in closer. "The secret ingredient is . . . *nothing*!"

"Huh?" Po asked.

"You heard me!" his father crowed. "There *is* no secret ingredient. To make something special, you just have to *believe* that it's special. It's all in the mind, son!"

Po just stared at his father for a moment in shock. Then he raised up the scroll tube and smiled serenely at his reflection on its surface. "There is no secret ingredient," he murmured.

Then Po looked up at the Jade Palace high on its majestic mountain.

Suddenly he understood the true secret of the scroll.

n the Jade Palace, Master Shifu
furiously fought against a giant,
muscular snow leopard: Tai Lung.
Both warriors were badly hurt, covered
in wounds and scorch marks, although
Shifu seemed to be in worse shape.

"Where is it?" Tai Lung hollered at
Shifu, slamming his old master to the
floor.

"The Dragon Warrior has taken the
scroll halfway across China by now,"
Shifu replied weakly. "You will never
see that scroll, Tai Lung."

Enraged, Tai Lung roared, preparing
to give Shifu a final blow.

"Hey!" Po called, out of breath from
climbing the stairs.

Tai Lung tossed Shifu aside and bounded over to Po. "Who are you?" he demanded.

"I'm the . . . ," Po replied, still short of breath, "Dragon Warrior."

"You?" the giant snow leopard jeered, laughing. "You're a panda. What are you going to do, sit on me?"

"No," Po answered, "I'm going to use *this*." He held up the Dragon Scroll.

Instantly, Tai Lung punched Po so hard that the panda flew across the room, and the scroll escaped from his grasp. "Finally," Tai Lung screeched, leaping for the scroll.

But Po bounced off a nearby pillar and slammed back into the snow leopard, snagging the scroll as he passed. Tai Lung chased Po as he ran toward the steps. The snow leopard quickly caught up with the panda, and they tumbled down the stairs together, Po still clinging to the scroll.

They crashed through the streets of the village. Both warriors scrambled for the scroll, battling for possession of it, kicking and pushing each other. Tai Lung hurled Po into a rock wall, and the scroll flew out of Po's paw again . . . and landed in the mouth of a carved dragon statue high on a rooftop.

Po concentrated, imagining there was a delicious cookie on the roof. Tai Lung gaped in amazement as Po effortlessly scaled the building. "The scroll has given him power!" Tai Lung growled. But before Po could reach the scroll, the snow leopard punched the side of the building with a massive blow, and the whole structure collapsed.

Amazingly, Po skipped down safely, bounding from falling tile to falling tile. As he neared the scroll again, Tai Lung lashed out with a devastating attack, smashing Po into the ground so forcefully that a nearby building toppled onto the panda.

As soon as the dust settled, Tai Lung grabbed the scroll. "Finally," he roared, "the power of the Dragon Scroll is mine!" He opened the tube and read the parchment inside.

"It's *nothing*!" Tai Lung growled.

Po climbed out of the rubble. "You don't get it, do you?" he said, pulling himself to his feet. "There is no secret ingredient. There's no magic and no miracles. It's just me."

With an evil snarl, Tai Lung launched himself at the panda. As he poked Po's nerve points with his claw, the panda just started to giggle—it tickled. "Stop! Stop it!" Po cried. "Don't!"

Roaring, Tai Lung delivered a wicked double-fisted punch to Po's belly. The shock wave rippled through Po's entire body. Po's arms flung out from the force and smacked Tai Lung, knocking the snow leopard back through the wall of the noodle shop.

Tai Lung attempted one more lunge at Po, but he just bounced off Po's enormous belly. The snow leopard was flung into the air, and he landed in a battered heap. "You can't . . . defeat me," Tai Lung snarled, breathing heavily. "You're just a big, fat panda!"

With lightning-fast speed, Po snagged Tai Lung's finger in a firm pinch. "I'm not a big, fat panda," Po replied. "I'm *the* big, fat panda."

"The Wuxi Finger Hold!" Tai Lung cried. "Shifu didn't teach you that!"

"Nope," Po said. "I figured it out myself."

He flexed his pinkie.

KA-THOOM!

A giant mushroom cloud appeared over the Valley of Peace.

Moments later, Po emerged from the cloud . . . looking very much like the great warrior from his kung fu dream. He wore a torn apron for a cape and an upside-down wok on his head.

"Look!" a villager cried. "The Dragon Warrior!" All the people cheered.

"That's my boy!" Po's father shouted. "That big, fat, lovely panda is my son!"

Po hugged his father as the Furious Five gathered around them. To Po's surprise, Tigress bowed deeply, followed by Mantis, Crane, Monkey, and Viper. "Master," Tigress said softly.

Po blushed. Then he remembered something. "Master Shifu!" he cried, as he raced back to the Jade Palace.

He climbed the stairs faster than ever before, but he was still breathless when he arrived at the palace doors. Shifu was lying on the floor with his eyes closed. "Master Shifu!" Po called. "Are you okay?"

Shifu's eyes fluttered open. "Po, you're alive," he whispered. "That or we're both dead."

"No, master," Po replied. "I didn't die. I defeated Tai Lung!"

Shifu smiled. "It is as Oogway foretold," he said softly. "You are the Dragon Warrior. You have brought peace to this valley, and to me. Thank you, Po . . ." The master's voice trailed off, and he closed his eyes again, his body becoming still.

"No, master!" Po sobbed. "Don't die, please!"

Shifu's eyes popped open. "I'm not dying, you idiot!" he snapped. "I mean . . . I'm not dying, Dragon Warrior. I'm simply one with the universe. Finally."

"Oh," Po said, lying down next to Shifu. "So,

um, I should stop talking?"

"If you can," Shifu replied.

Po nodded reverently as Shifu closed his eyes again. Soft wind chimes tinkled in the distance, clinking in the gentle breeze.

"Want to get something to eat?" Po asked.

Shifu sighed. "Yeah."